Family Matters

Gaurav Monga

Family Matters
by Gaurav Monga
ISBN: 978-1-908125-67-5

Cover Art by David Rix

Publication Date: February 2019

Contents

My father named himself. My Grandfather was an exceptionally forward thinking man who hated going to the temple. He said, "why not let the child name himself". My father grew fond of the Lone Ranger, the western film hero, and when he was five years old, he rolled up to his father, asking him if he could be called that. My dad, from that day onward, was called Lone Ranger Monga. I was Baba and my younger brother was Bapi. I was five and he was two when we were finally named. I remember seeing birthday cakes in the shape of big B's until then. The accountant wanted to open bank accounts in our names and told my parents that they could call me Gaurav and the younger one could be called Saurabh, for now at least. They could always change their names when they grow up......

The Family Nose

When my brother was born, he was just a nose in a hospital bed amongst many babies. The doctors pointed him out, tucked in the sheets. The nose was as large as my brother. My parents knew how this would turn out; babies are not as tall as noses but with time my brother grew and, at his full height, his nose began sticking out, no matter how much he tried to cover it.

He didn't attract women and often people, reaching a dead end in an argument with him, would say, "You're nothing but a nose."

At college, he finally met someone who fell in love with his nose. For some reason she loved noses of all sizes, though she didn't have a particularly prominent one, herself. She loved to play with his.

He would often get annoyed at this behaviour, but tolerated it because he knew that not many people loved him.

One day while she was fast asleep, my brother tottered out of bed, swaying his hips from left to right. He tripped on an electric wire; his nose came off. My brother, in his extreme joy, shouted out, waking up his girlfriend, who rolled out of bed. He expected her to notice immediately but when she didn't, he picked up the broken nose and paraded it in front of her eyes.

My brother still had a nose on, however. Clearly, underneath that nose was another one. He tried tripping on the same electric wire, but didn't fall this time. Instead the wire got tangled around his legs and he needed to spend the whole night untangling it without his girlfriend there.

My sister had a child. She didn't seem to have a nose at all, which worried the family elders, so much so that they said the child was not hers; well, of course a woman with such a formidable nose ought to have a daughter with a nose at least half as promising as her mother's. What the elders didn't know was that my sister had secret intercourse with a noseless man, something the elders could have never imagined.

My father was born with a hooked-nose. When he was twenty years old, he tried to get the hook removed via surgery. The surgery was a sore failure and my father had to cancel his trip to the

United States of America because they had to tie a bandage over it. Till today, my father cannot smell or breathe through it.

My mother has a perfect nose.

I would talk about my wife, who likes to pick her nose, but I am not married yet and live at home with my parents and siblings.

My nose is, of course, very different, because I am the middle child. As the middle child, it has always been easy for me to look at my family from a more removed perspective, as if I have slipped out of its centre.

Little Box

Pasted on the wall opposite her desk was a sheet of ruled paper on which was written *Daddy*. I didn't give it much importance as I walked in after a tiring day. My wife had been talking about her father a lot for the last six months, saying that her father would do this for her, her father would do that for her. I lounged on my bed and, a moment later, she appeared in the living room with a glass of hot water in her hand. She sat at her desk and stared into this piece of paper, which I had forgotten all about. She roamed around the room and sat on the other bed, perpendicular to the one I had been lolling on. "I spoke to him today." She pointed her chin towards the sheet of paper on the wall. "And he told me," she pointed at it again and looked at me, "that I should come and see him in Germany and that you could eventually find a job there."

"What would you do?" I asked her. She said that he – she turned her head, facing the sheet of paper – would figure something out for her. I walked over to the paper and pointed at it with my index finger, saying, "Don't be too sure. What if, once you get there, he tells everyone that he's not your father, huh?"

I moved away from the table and sat on the chair. The word *daddy* was written in golden brown marker. The handwriting resembled the one I had seen in her father's letters to her. "Did he send you this sheet of paper?" No, but when he was visiting last, he carefully took it out of a little box.

She then told me that her father was arriving tomorrow, and that hopefully he would take us back with him to Germany.

Daddy arrived today – all his luggage stuffed in boxes. He took out his navy blue coat and hung it on a nail that couldn't carry its weight. On his way to the bathroom, later on, he found that his coat had fallen to the floor. He picked it up, dusted it, put it on and stared at himself in the mirror, which was when I showed up. I was standing behind daddy, and daddy and I were both looking at ourselves in the mirror.

Daddy loved his little daughter, whom he liked to call his little box because he liked to take her everywhere. Truly, in all of the little time her father spent at our home, I found myself sitting alone for most of it, sipping some terrible tea. The only time I saw him was when he came to wish me goodnight.

Before you knew it, daddy had taken his little box – along with all the other boxes – to Germany. I was supposed to follow.

I went home, swinging my arms, kind of happy, left to my own devices. In a few days, however, I got bored and started masturbating to boring porn. I told myself that this would all end when she returned.

I would sit at the desk and stare at the sheet of paper whilst sipping on tea. I had ripped it off the wall and would examine it closely to have something to do while drinking tea. I had put a box on the desk. The box was so little nothing could fit inside.

While daddy was taking his little box across Europe, I was trying to get the tailor to alter the navy blue coat to fit me. I thought my wife would like it on me when she returned in the winter.

The Trees

The park had a running track and, on an elevated climb, bushes sat plump, round and cropped.

He had asked her to meet him at one of the benches near the track. She sat there, looking around and then at the round, plump green bushes. She almost thought she saw him hiding behind one of them. She ventured up the steps and even looked inside some of the bushes, while he was hiding behind the tall wooden trees next to the track, trying to shoo away the little children who were hugging his legs.

She thought she must have been going crazy looking for a man behind a tree when all she saw was a little boy clinging to the tree's trunk.

She went back to the bench. She loosened her neck. She sat and scanned the whole park for this man who was everywhere. Her face had gone red.

When she finally left, he emerged from a bush – leaves and dirt in his hair. He looked down at the bench and thought of what it would be like to sit there. Now that he didn't need to hide behind the trees anymore.

The English Teacher

Even if my clothes are dirty, I know that all I need to do is take them off to be good again, because my body is fine, and now all that I need to do is to put some fresh clothes on...

We stood in the library. We were not naked but we might as well have been. We were waiting for the teacher to arrive. She arrived late, only a few minutes before the bell rang, saying that there was an emergency of some kind. None of us complained to the principal. I loved her classes when she came. She was a mediocre teacher and though she was a little boring, she could also appear fresh and ready to teach. Our school was so large that no one ever found out she often used to miss most of the lesson.

I am a big boy, I used to think to myself, but when I grew older I realized that there were many boys and girls bigger than me. When I become an adult, I used to think to myself, I would become a very average, mediocre writer, writing stories whose endings are well known before they happen, and I will be very content with my life, finding readers who like average stories, readers who like to feel average and mediocre about themselves. This feeling gives many, including me, much strength.

In the evenings I like to go for long walks around the school football field, while my friend runs around the track. I walk calmly, watching the sunset. I am fat and love to eat, especially sweets. When I was younger I used to take pride in my round shape. I used to take pride in the fact that it took me longer to get into a boat when we visited the lake. I used to even dress like an older fat man, wearing navy blue and grey cardigans on a rainy, slightly cold day. Today I am ashamed of the fat on my stomach. I want to be like my friend, but I am much too lazy and useless to go on a diet and begin exercising. I am clearly a big boy, almost a child with the body of a grown-up fat man.

I fell in love with my English teacher in my last year of school. She liked to drink coffee at breakfast. I poured myself a cup, knowing that coffee unnecessarily stimulates my nerves, and went and sat with her. She told me that I would one day be an average, mediocre writer. I told her it didn't matter to anyone what sort of writer I would be. I just needed to be a good person. She was surprised at my simplicity and took me home. I didn't know what to do with my English teacher. She read me a story and I went to sleep.

The next day we went to school together. There was a group of people gathered around the principal's office, playing football. It looked silly and we all laughed. A few minutes later, the principal, himself, came out in shorts and T-shirt.

Later, I left my dorm room and found a group of people running towards me. They looked like monkeys and I felt scared. They ran past me. It was only when I reached the main school block did I understand why they looked like monkeys. The school building had burnt down. The English teacher had gone missing.

A few days later I graduated from school. We smoked cigars at the graduation ceremony. I soon left town, forgetting the school and my friend. The only image I had in my mind, when my parents picked me up from the airport and asked how the graduation ceremony had been, was of my English teacher, bathing in the sun on the terrace of her impoverished house.

Missing Gautam

He received a text message from a woman addressing him as a certain Gautam Uncle, telling him that a taxi driver would be waiting for him at the airport on his arrival. A few minutes later he received a call from the taxi driver, himself, who insisted that even if he was not Gautam Uncle, he must be waiting at the airport for a taxi. He said that he was lying on his bed. Then the woman herself called to speak to Gautam Uncle, to which he replied that he was not Gautam Uncle, at all.

While taking a shower, he thought that perhaps he was Gautam Uncle after all, maybe not completely but in some small way. When they called again, he told both of them that he most certainly was Gautam Uncle; it was just that he was not waiting at the airport but was at home having breakfast with his mother.

They stormed into his apartment to find out whether this was true, both the woman and the taxi driver. The taxi driver could never have been sure. He had never seen Gautam Uncle before, and as for the woman, she hadn't either. And so they took Gautam Uncle away.

It had grown dark. His mother, her jaws hanging open, still sat at the dining table, trying to figure out in her own head where her Gautam had gone.

Running Away From Ranjan

Running away from Ranjan while living in the same city involves trying to avoid speaking in the same voice as his in situations where people might sense that you are his son.

Running away from Ranjan is not easy given that Ranjan is whom you are running away from.

While running away from Ranjan, one can always resort to rowing a boat down a river to safety.

It often involves ducking your head in places in his neighbourhood that you are visiting right now with Ranjan that Ranjan didn't know you had visited only a day before without him.

It also means ignoring all that you have in common with him, only because you want to run away.

Running away from Ranjan in the park means hiding behind tall trees while he is walking by; if you are with a friend, let the friend walk on with a straight face, as if he were not with you at all.

*

Running away from Ranjan means not demonstrating Ranjan-like characteristics to your new girlfriend on the first day, for she might run away from you, too.

Everyone I know seems to be running away from Ranjan. I wonder why. Even the ones who act as though they are not are running away from him.

Running away from Ranjan means hoping that the same neuroses you share with him – though in a more minor, benign way – won't grow.

When Ranjan visits you in the town you work at and catches you by surprise in the lobby of your apartment building, invite him in and show him to his room. Then invite your closest friends, and don't feel embarrassed by what he has to say about your childhood.

Even if they are lies, he knows that your friends know you better, and sooner or later Ranjan will feel ashamed and will hopefully become silent of his own accord.

Last year, you stopped by your hometown on Ranjan's birthday and took him out for lunch to a fancy restaurant that was admittedly uncomfortable right after the eating. You did not know where to take him, especially after he was asking you to take notes of all the potential business plans he had panned out for you. You took him to the home of your friend, who was not there at the time, and after having a few cups of tea, you signalled for Ranjan to leave. Ranjan threw the little money you lent him in your face, called your mother a cunt, and left. This time, Ranjan ran away from you.

Occasionally Ranjan might visit you in disguise. Don't, however, forget that he is your father.

In Ranjan's universe, everyone is sick. You will never be able to prove to Ranjan that you are doing well. He will always be able to find something wrong with you and might even convince you of it. He will call your doctors and their assistants, and they will start running away from him, too.

Ranjan often contends that things would have turned out quite differently for him if only he had not taken the wrong medicines.

How many will it take to run away from him before he realises it?

Instead, he has people running after you.

I don't really want to run away from Ranjan. In fact, I want to stay close to his woman-like bosom. I just wish he would understand. Perhaps, I need to write him a letter, telling him that he does not need to chase me. Going through my e-mails to him, I realise that I have written this letter many times before.

Whilst reading my first experiment with the short story, Ranjan found that the protagonist's father was much like him. He refused to read the story to its end. Instead he found fault in the more formal aspects and asked me to first learn English.

In the early days of running away, I first moved to the southernmost tip of the subcontinent, to landscapes that didn't remind me of him.

There also was a time when he wanted you to run away, and when you visited him in his falling-apart house, he didn't open the door.

Running away from Ranjan is as difficult as it is to not run away from him. Ranjan ensures that. While talking to him, he often assumes a persona presupposing that all the running away was never really worth your effort. This is somehow comforting, for this is what you wanted in the first place – but as a result of all those lost years, he treats you like a fifteen year old boy.

In his path forward, he visits all his old haunts and his failed watch shop almost every day, imagining the future trapped in an eternally recurring past.

He goes through old matters with old friends, re-enacting real lived moments that happened between them in the 80s. Those friends often get in touch with you, asking you not to share their phone numbers with him, asking whether it would be alright with you if they ran away from Ranjan, too.

Running away from Ranjan is often embarrassing and ruins your health, though that is all he seems to be ostensibly concerned about. He knows you are unwell, but always suspects the wrong symptom. He keeps going on about your grey hair when all along it is your stomach that is in need of repair.

Perhaps my problems with Ranjan have nothing to do with Ranjan, per se. Perhaps they are my own insecurities projected on to the tapestry of my father. Poor Ranjan, what did he do to deserve such a son.

Photographs

After the divorce, dad cut mother out of all the memories. Even those moments when she was holding me. With mother gone, I was left suspended in the air.

When I asked dad why he had cut her out, his only response was that there were many people in the house who were good with scissors.

I wonder whether I am telling the truth about him.

My sister showed me some pictures where I could not find her. She said she was hidden somewhere inside the folds.

I didn't understand their grief. Instead, I flipped through photographs – each funeral had its own album – and although both funerals had a lot in common, the people present in the chapel that day cried differently.

Dear mom and dad, I know you hate each other and have not spoken to each other in many years. Today I get married, and if nothing else, can you at least pose like you did on the day of your own wedding.

We have been collecting memories of people who accidentally came to mind for some time now.

A servant, not knowing who these people were,
juxtaposed their faces with those who were dear,
resulting in a collage. My brother decided one day
to tidy up the house and cut out the faces of the
dear ones by mistake.

Clown

In the centre of this story is a clown. That, in itself, is not particularly funny. There are many stories with clowns in them. In fact, too many. The only difference here is that the clown happens to be your father........

But at least you find me funny.

Yeah dad, but I don't want to have a father who is a clown

Dad then told me about the time he decided to join the circus.

"On stage, I often used to depict a failed businessman. The crowd clearly found a clown taking business seriously funny. Your mother didn't laugh. She, in fact, didn't talk to me, which was when I left the circus and your mother by then had already started a school for little children. I asked her if I could at least become the school jester, make the children laugh during their breaks. Your mother did not think it was an altogether bad idea. Instead of doing the act of the failed businessman, I did the failed student, you know the kind that stays on in the same grade so he obviously looks much older than his peers. I would sit in the corner when the principal would walk by.

"Once they started shouting in the hallways, Call the clown, call the clown.

"Your mother had called me into her office. I even tried to discuss you, but she said that she didn't want to mix the personal with the professional, and then told me that my depiction of the failing student represented a fall she was not keen to endorse. I told her it was a joke, and besides, school grades don't really decide where you end up anyway. Look at me, I was a college topper."

While the children were in class, my father was instructed to assist the gardener in watering the plants and during holidays he assisted anyone in need, all the time wearing a costume and a prosthetic nose that looked like the nose he had in his younger days. No one ever found out that he was my father, even when I paid visits to pick up my mother from school. Even he, himself, hesitated to acknowledge it. Slowly, children stopped laughing at his jokes because they were always the same ones and over time, my father became, as a result, more and more inconspicuous and vanished into the everyday life of his work place.

www.ingramcontent.com/pod-product-compliance
Lightning Source LLC
Chambersburg PA
CBHW030403200726

48286CB00015B/2788